DAGWYN

the Very

GOOD DRAGON

SUSAN GROO

PAGE PUBLISHING, INC.
New York, NY

First originally published by Page Publishing, Inc. 2016

ISBN 978-1-68213-855-7 (hbk)
ISBN 978-1-68213-856-4 (digital)

Printed in the United States of America

FOR BRANDON

Dagwyn, the fire-breathing dragon
Had always been misunderstood,
Though he fumed and he siz-
zled and spit plumes of flame,
His every intention was good.

He'd once, long ago, left
his cave by the sea
And traveled inland to the town,
But the residents there saw
the fiery flare of his breath
And they chased him back down.

Many times, he put on his
tie and his top hat
then marched into town with a smile.
See? He was no mon-
ster who wanted to fight;
He just wanted to visit a while.

The townspeople couldn't
get over their fright.
They'd see his fire-breath, and they'd hide.
Nobody would talk to him,
no one would listen;
They just screamed and they all ran inside.

Not one person would give him
a chance for a minute;
They thought he was all teeth and claws.
So Dagwyn gave up 'cause
they wouldn't give in
And see what a great guy he was.

The children threw rocks, called
him names, and were cruel;
Grown-ups acted hateful and mean.
Dagwyn ran to his den, afraid of the men,
Terrified to be heard, smelled, or seen.

Back at the beach, Dagwyn
kept to himself,
Took long walks on the shore all alone.
He had only himself to
keep company with,
No neighbors, no e-mails, no phone.

Poor Dagwyn was lone-
some, he needed a friend,
Somebody who'd look past the smoke,
Somebody to love him,
somebody to care,
With whom he could laugh,
play, and joke.

But days turned to weeks and
months turned to years;
Nobody would venture to come
To the caverns down by
the side of the sea,
Near the place that the
dragon called "home".

Then, one day as Dagwyn
moped, dismally sad,
A noise came from outside his cave.
"Who's out there?" he cried,
he was so very scared,
But was hoping to sound *really* brave.

Dagwyn crept to the mouth
of his cave, tippy-toed,
Hoping against hope that he'd find
Someone come to visit and
not come to hurt,
A friendly face, gentle and kind.

A boy! A freckle-faced, barefooted boy,
With bucket and shovel in hand,
Stood gaping and grin-
ning, his smile ear-to-ear,
His shoulders and bare feet were tanned.

His family had come from the city
To spend a few days in the sun;
But Darby ran off from the rest of the crowd,
In search of adventure and fun.

Though he saw all the fire and
felt Dagwyn's hot breath,
Darby said that he wasn't afraid;
They ran and they frolicked,
Built castles of sand;
For hours and hours they played.

Sharing their hopes, fears and
dreams for the future,
They knew what a bond
they had made.
Dagwyn sat himself down
on the warm, salty sand
So his new friend could
nap in his "shade".

"A friend! What a wonder-
ful, beautiful thing!"
Dagwyn thought, as the little boy slept,
But his secret, this fire-blow-
ing, flame-throwing thing,
From all others still had to be kept.

Darby woke with a smile
as bright as the sun,
And told Dagwyn that he had dreamed
Of the most perfect way to
save Dagwyn's day;
and things weren't as bad
as they seemed.

"I dreamed of a fireman who
told me," said Darby,
(and he sees problems like
yours every day),
'No magical potion, just a
HUGE gulp of ocean
Will wash your flame-troubles away!' "

"Can you swim?" asked the
boy of the dragon,
"Have you ever swum in the ocean?"
"Why, no," answered Dagwyn,
"Although I *can* swim,
I've never had any such notion."

"I don't *want* to get soggy,
take my feet off dry land,
Or to go out and play with the fishes.
But, if swimming it takes,
then swimming I'll do
To satisfy my deepest wishes!"

"I want people to love me
and not be afraid,
I want to be known for good works.
No more will they run and in
great terror shun me
Because of my fiery quirks!"

So together they walked
out onto the beach,
Boy and dragon, best
pals, trusting friends,
"Go on, now. I promise I'll
wait here for you here,
And I'll love you *however* this ends."

Dagwyn waved to his friend
and dived into the surf,
He swam far, far out from the shore,
Then he lowered his head, sank
down into the depths,
And he drank and he drank,
yet, some more.

With his tummy all filled up with water,
He looked like a giant balloon,
But he felt a new cooling sensation inside,
and his heartburn? It won't return soon!

He coughed and he sput-
tered, but nary a flame,
Neither flicker nor spark nor an ember;
Only hisses of steam issued
forth from his mouth.
And the fire? Soon, no one will remember!

Through June and July, they
made friends at the beach;
People learned Dagwyn wasn't a threat.
Soon all of the youngsters and
some of the oldsters
Were having their best summer yet!

The beach-goers watched in amazement
As the dragon gave rides on his back.

Dagwyn gave swimming les-
sons, he surfed like a pro,
And for diving, he had quite a knack.

As August rolled 'round and
summer wound down,
The circle of friends grew and grew.
The townsfolk were happy and
they all loved Dagwyn
who was happy 'cause loved THEM, too.

What?? Us hate dear Dagwyn?
Could've *never* been true!
He's the one who'll be true to the end.
He's gentle and kind, he's
caring and COOL,
And he owes all that he is to his friend.

Though the summer went fast,
these friendships would last,
Dagwyn knew that he'd no more be lonely.
He just wished that Darby
could stay with him here
And live in his cave. Yes, if only....

But school would soon open
and all boys must go
To keep up their important studies.
So he put on a grin and they
took their last swim
Knowing always, they would be best buddies.

When Darby went back to
his home in the city,
Dagwyn thought that his
big heart would break,
But they'd promised each other
they'd meet every summer,
No matter what it may take.

They'd come back together
to have some more fun,
To share secrets, to grow and mature,
And year after year, they'd
both return here,
Where their friendship
began at the shore.

About the Author

Having begun writing poems, stories and books for her thirteen grandchildren, Susan Groo is now sharing those stories for the enjoyment of everyone's children and grandchildren. She currently lives in Georgia with her husband and her cockapoo, Mojo.

CPSIA information can be obtained
at www.ICGtesting.com
Printed in the USA
LVOW06*0728271116

514617LV00014B/126/P

9 781682 138557